THE CHRISTMAS CORPSE

A HOT DOG DETECTIVE MYSTERY HOLIDAY NOVELLA

MATHIYA ADAMS

Misque Press

ABOUT THE CHRISTMAS CORPSE

When Santa turns up dead in a Christmas Tree lot, things look bad for Christmas. Especially since the man playing Santa who was working at the lot over the holidays was a friend from his homeless days.

Someone is definitely not feeling the Christmas spirit and MacFarland's other homeless friends may be the next to die...

DEDICATION

Dedicated to my daughters, Laura, Lisa, and Tina and to my son Kevin, for all the joy they've brought me throughout their lives.

ALSO BY MATHIYA ADAMS

NOVELS IN THE CRYSTAL COVE SERIES

The Ghost on the Stairs
The Ghost in the Ice House (Coming Soon)
The Ghost in the Vineyard (Coming Soon)

NOVELS IN THE HOT DOG DETECTIVE SERIES

The Avid Angler
The Busty Ballbreaker
The Crying Camper
The Desperate Druggie
The Eager Evangelist
The Freaky Fan
The Groping Gardener
The Harried Hairdresser
The Impetuous Intruder
The Jaded Jezebel
The Kitchen Khemist

The Lazy Lawyer
The Morose Mistress
The Naughty Neighbor
The Obnoxious Oilman
The Paranoid Patient
The Quibbling Quartet
The Remorseful Rafter
The Strident Student
The Truculent Trannie
The Unselfish Uncle
The Vacillating Vigilante
The Wasted Womanizer
The Xanthic Xena
The Young Yogi
The Zamboni Zealot
The Absent Ally

Novellas

The Christmas Corpse
The Easter Evader
The Jovial Juror

Sign up for my newsletter, with stories about upcoming books, by emailing Mathiya Adams at Misque Press: editor@misquepress.com or at www.mathiyaadams.com.

If you have any suggestions, compliments, criticisms or wish to write a review, please feel free to contact me directly at Mathiya.Adams@gmail.com.

I look forward to hearing from you.

ZAYNE CORTLAND RACED between the rows of Christmas trees, laughing wildly. None of rows matched up with the lanes and markings of the original parking lot where Caleb's Christmas Trees was located, but that didn't matter to five-and-a-half-year-old Zayne.

Zayne knew it wasn't a good idea to get Santa upset with him, but it was too late for that. Yesterday, Santa had yelled at him for no reason at all. Zayne had just been playing Super Jet versus Killer Robot Trees. He hadn't *meant* to bump into anybody. Or knock over a wreath. Or pull Santa's beard. Well, okay, he meant to do that, but only because he wanted to see if it would come off. It had looked funny, a little lopsided, and like it didn't quite match Santa's dark brown skin.

As he passed a Christmas tree, Zayne tore off a shiny red tag, angled like a Super Jet, and flew it through the lot, making shooting sounds. *Pwew! Pwew! Pwew!* Then: *Bang!* One of the Killer Robot Trees shot back! Super Jet went down! Zayne let the red tag flutter to the snow-covered wood chips that had been spread on the ground. Zayne laughed and sped around a corner.

And stopped.

Santa was lying in his path.

Zayne forgot about the battle. He walked cautiously over to Santa's body. Was this a trick? Santa might be playing a game. Didn't reindeer play games? Santa probably did too. Maybe he was pretending he'd been shot down by Super Jet and when Zayne got close, Santa would jump up and scare him! But Zayne was too smart for that. He wasn't afraid at all. He wasn't a little kid, he was *almost six years old!* Nothing scared him!

As Zayne neared Santa's body, he watched for any movement, but Santa was as still as a mouse. He got close to the body and kicked Santa, to see what reaction he might get.

None.

Santa was lying on his side, his back to Zayne. The young boy moved cautiously around to the Santa's front. The first thing Zayne noticed was that it was the Santa from yesterday, who had yelled at him.

The second thing Zayne noticed was the pool of blood near Santa's head.

Zayne started screaming, "Santa's dead! Santa's dead! Somebody killed Santa!"

Five days earlier...

"IT'S remarkable that they got this house ready in time for Thanksgiving," said MacFarland, looking around at the sparse furnishings. "Maybe we can help you get more furniture."

Gracie nodded. "Yes, that would be nice, but wait a week or two. The church is going to bring some donations in next week." Seeing MacFarland's dubious look, she quickly added. "Don't worry, Mac, this house isn't part of the Church of Blessed Grace. It's supported by Catholic Charities and some private donors."

MacFarland laughed. "I was pretty sure that at least you and Kirk wouldn't get involved with that shady group again."

Gracie, as was typical for her ebullient nature, assumed the role of spokesperson for the six homeless people living in the remodeled home. "We wanted to make our own Thanksgiving dinner, but instead, one of the shelters is giving it to us. It should be here any minute. Meanwhile, we've made do with what we have."

She laughed and waved at the table set up in the dining room. It had one candle in the middle of the table, surrounded by boughs of a fir tree, pine cones, and red berries. Eight place settings circled the table. Nothing fancy. Only a few of the plates matched. But the esthetics of the decor didn't matter. What mattered was that six homeless people had shelter and a place to call home.

MacFarland studied the group, an old habit he picked up from his days on the Denver Police force. MacFarland still retained the rock hard, compact body he had developed as a Marine and retained as a cop. He had lost that job when he took up drinking, trying to hide from the death of his wife. While on the street, he had befriended Rufus Headley, a Vietnam vet who looked out for MacFarland.

Now, he and Rufus were about to share Thanksgiving dinner with a group of former homeless people. MacFarland had seen most of these people on the street, before they had been given the opportunity to live in this refurbished house. He had to admit though that of all six homeless people, he only really knew Kirk and Gracie. Kirk was a bear of a man, silent, constantly hovering near Gracie's side, protectively guarding her from all threats and dangers.

MacFarland coughed. "Gracie, this is a bit embarrassing, but I haven't been on the streets in several years. I recognize Leroy, but I'm afraid I don't know these other people."

Leroy, a young man of twenty-five years, introduced the others. "Mac, this is Harry."

Harry was an older man, perhaps in his thirties.

Harry was pot-bellied and had a considerable slouch, whether from gravity or fatigue, MacFarland could not tell. Harry stuck out his hand, and MacFarland shook it. Not a strong handshake, but one which confidence had deserted.

"This is Ozzie. Me and Ozzie are old friends."

Ozzie was a black man in his late twenties, tall and lanky, a spindly type of person. "Hiya, Mac, nice to meet you."

"And finally, this is Gloria."

Gloria proved to be a tired woman in her late thirties with an alarming skin condition. MacFarland hoped she was getting medical treatment for what looked like a bad case of shingles, but he was hesitant to bring the subject up. Surely the people who were sponsoring these homeless folk had looked into treatment options.

Rufus didn't need to be introduced. It appeared that Rufus knew everyone, and everyone knew Rufus.

No sooner had introductions been made than the promised dinner arrived. The turkey came in a large aluminum roasting pan, the side dishes in various containers. "You may have to reheat everything," said the young man who carried the dinner in from the street.

"I've already got the oven pre-heated," said Gracie. "Besides, it helped warm up the kitchen."

Within an hour, all of them were seated around the table. Kirk was unanimously volunteered to be the "Papa" and carve the turkey, a task he seemed to relish. When everyone had their plates piled high with turkey, dressing, squash, peas and onions, cranberry sauce, and mashed potatoes with gravy, Gracie offered a prayer.

"Good Lord, we thank you for this unexpected bounty, and while some of us--" she looked at Harry sternly "--have taken your name in vain, we've never lost sight of the fact that you have always had our backs. And we are thankful that You've finally decided to put a roof over our heads."

Most of the group uttered Amen, except for Ozzie, who looked a bit bemused. Leroy saw his friend's expression and offered a quick explanation. "Ozzie is a Muslim, but I'm sure he shares the sentiments Gracie said."

Ozzie nodded quickly. "I do, I do. May Allah Be Praised."

"Well, then," said Kirk in a rare display of loquaciousness, "Let's dig in!"

When dinner was finally over, Gracie and Gloria served coffee and cookies to everyone. As MacFarland drank his coffee, he looked over at Kirk and Gracie. "Now that you have a real house to live in, does that mean I'm not going to see you at my cart anymore?"

MacFarland operated a hot dog cart. Having once been homeless, he never forgot how many times he'd gone hungry. He made a habit of providing free food to any homeless person who came to his cart.

Kirk and Gracie looked at each other. Some silent communication must have passed between them. Then Gracie spoke for the couple. "We'll still come around, Mac. We might not be as desperate for food, but you still have the best hot dogs in Denver."

"You mean the best cheesy hot dogs, don't you?" asked Rufus. "The cheese was my idea."

Gracie smiled. "Yes, and the best cheesy dogs too. We

could never forget all that both of you have done for us. We are so thankful for everything that you've sacrificed for us and so many others."

MacFarland smiled. "It's not a sacrifice when it's something you want to do. I am just thankful that I have always had so many wonderful friends to count on. You may not have had a roof over your head, but you have a good heart."

"Hey, I got an idea," said Rufus. "Why don't we all go around and say what we're thankful for this holiday season?"

Gracie looked over at Kirk. "We'll start. Kirk says he is grateful that our health has been good. He was really worried when I had to go into the hospital earlier this year. Remember, Mac, you drove me there. As for me, I'm grateful that I have Kirk to take care of. I don't know what I would do with my life if I didn't have him around to take care of."

MacFarland had always thought that it was Kirk who took care of Gracie, but maybe it worked both ways.

Leroy raised his hand. "I am grateful that I got friends like Rufus...and you too, Mac. And now that I have a place to live, I'm going to find a job so that I can get back on my feet."

Gloria looked around the table with an uncertain expression. "I'm not sure what I'm thankful for. I guess maybe it's that you all let me live with you."

"I'm grateful for lots of things, but here's what I want for Christmas," said Ozzie. "Even though I'm Muslim, I think that Santa Claus brings presents to everyone, even Muslims. But you have to ask for what you want, right?

So I'm asking Santa to help Gloria get rid of her shingles."

Gloria was surprised by Ozzie's statement, but smiled at him. She turned to the last member of their group. "Harry, what do you want for Christmas?"

Harry shook his head. "Doesn't matter. Not going to happen." After a moment, he burst out sarcastically, "Why doesn't Santa ever bring anything people actually want? Screw presents. You know what would be a good Christmas present? Money, that's what. Cold, hard cash."

It was supposed to be a joke, but Harry sounded angry and bitter.

"Harry will be playing the part of Scrooge this year," Gloria smirked.

Gracie wasn't amused. She glared at Harry.

After Harry wandered away from the group, Rufus said to MacFarland, "He hasn't seen his wife and kids in a while. He feels worst about it around Christmas."

CHAPTER TWO
SUNDAY, NOVEMBER 26, 0850 HOURS

SANTA CLAUSE RAN up to the hot dog stand at the corner of Fourteenth Avenue and Elati Street, across the street from the courthouse and the jail. When Santa stood in front of MacFarland and Rufus, who were manning the stand, he turned out to be familiar.

"I told you I would get a job," said Leroy, unable to contain his excitement. He gestured to the red suit with pride.

"That's great Leroy. Why are you dressed as Santa? Where are you working?"

"At a Christmas tree lot a couple of blocks from here. The guy who owns the parking lot sells Christmas trees every year there. He hired me for the season. He makes us dress up like Santa or one of his elves. We get to rotate who will be Santa. No one likes being Santa, since we have to wear pillows to make us fat and it's hard to work when you're wearing a pillow. So usually the new guy gets the red suit. I'd rather be Santa than an elf though, because elves have to wear these girly green tights."

MacFarland did not feel it was appropriate to point out that the season would only last a month. Hopefully Leroy already was aware of that fact. "So you started yesterday?"

"Yep. I been there one day, and already I sold ten trees. But mostly, I set up. The trees come in on a big truck, so I have to unload them, put a stand on them, and place them so customers can view them. It's not hard work, except for the pillows, but my boss, Caleb, is always yelling. Now there's someone who should get the Christmas spirit!"

"I've used his parking lot a couple of times. Only ran into him once or twice. He never struck me as very friendly."

"His wife works during the days, and she complains even more than he does. They really are made for each other, you know? Two peas in a pod or something like that. He keeps saying that he'd like to get someone to replace her. I'm going to see if he will hire Ozzie to take her place. Her name is Roxy or something."

"But you do enjoy working there, don't you?"

"Yes and no. I thought at first that I was going to get paid by the hour, but Caleb said no. He pays me a daily amount, and then I get one dollar for each tree I sell. I like working nights, because that's when most of the customers come by, between three in the afternoon and nine at night. After that, it's really quiet."

"How late do you work?"

"Until about midnight. He's got a fence around the place and I have to make sure it's locked up. Apparently the Christmas tree business is really a cutthroat business. Who would have thought? I mean, it's the Christmas season, you know? Good cheer and all that. But Caleb says that some lot owners pay people to sabotage other guy's trees. It's a bloodthirsty business if you ask me."

"You ain't doing any of that, are you?" asked Rufus. "The sabotaging, I mean."

Leroy looked shocked. "No, not me. I don't want to lose my house. If I get into trouble with the cops, I get taken off the list and I'm back on the streets. I'm not going to risk that, not for some damn Christmas trees." Leroy became thoughtful. "He does get some of the others to do things like that, so maybe he might ask me. But I won't do it."

"Do you really think you can get Ozzie a job?" asked MacFarland.

"Sure do. That woman, Roxy, she just complains all day long. Drives me and the other three people who work there crazy. I know it drives Caleb crazy, because he is always threatening to beat the crap out of her if she don't stop complaining. But she don't stop. I think she likes to pull his chain."

Rufus scratched his beard. "So how long is this job gonna last?"

"Just until Christmas. Maybe a day or two after, to clean up the lot. Caleb said last year they got their last shipment of trees in late and couldn't sell them. That's what Roxy is always complaining about. How much money they lost last year. But Caleb keeps telling her that she should shut the fuck up and get some Christmas spirit." Leroy smiled. "Guess he has all the Christmas spirit in the family."

"I wonder where they get their trees," mused Rufus.

"They must have tree farms up in the mountains," offered MacFarland.

Leroy nodded. "Yeah, they buy the trees up north. Don't know if it's in Colorado or Wyoming, It's the brother who gets the trees. He comes down in a rented truck every couple of days with about a hundred trees."

"You gonna sell that many?"

"Hope so," laughed Leroy. "More trees I sell, the more I make! Or at least I will make it if Caleb don't drive me crazy first."

MacFarland smiled. "I thought it was Roxy who drove you crazy."

"Oh, it is. But Caleb, he got his own way of being a prick. When the truck comes in, he has to examine every tree there is."

"What's he looking for?"

"I suppose to make sure the tree has the right label. We got a lot of varieties. Balsam Fir, Douglas Fir, Noble Fir, Scotch Pine, and Blue Spruce. I still can't recognize all of them right away, but Caleb does seem to know his trees. Or maybe he don't. I can't tell, but he sure sounds convincing, and he makes customers believe that whatever tree they are buying is the best one for them."

"You know more about those trees than I do," observed Rufus. "I didn't even know there was that many types."

"We also will flock the trees for you, with different

colors. Pink. Blue. Silver. We even did a rainbow tree for this one gay couple. They were really appreciative."

"Maybe we'll come by and get a tree for Cyn's house," said MacFarland. "Though I haven't seen her put up a tree in the past. I wonder...could she be the Grinch?"

LEROY, this time dressed in the green tights, ran up to MacFarland's hot dog cart. "Mac! Mac! You hafta come over to the tree lot!"

"Calm down, Leroy, what's the problem?"

"There's been a terrible accident! Or worse! Over at the tree lot, come on!"

MacFarland and Rufus exchanged looks, and Rufus slowly nodded. MacFarland followed Leroy the two blocks to the parking lot where Caleb had his Christmas tree lot.

What he found surprised him. Half a dozen police cars were parked along the street or on the lot, lights flashing. A small crowd of on-lookers gawked at the commotion in the tree lot. An ambulance was just pulling away. MacFarland spied Benny Lockwood, a detective with the Denver Police Department, and one of MacFarland's closest friends. He and Leroy walked towards the back of the lot. A policeman stopped them. MacFarland pointed towards the detective. "We're with him," he said.

Lockwood stood up as MacFarland and Leroy came near. Lockwood was tall and lanky, a modern day Abraham Lincoln, even affecting clothes that didn't quite fit him.

"What's happening, Benny?"

"Black man, dressed in a Santa outfit, late twenties, one forty pounds, six feet tall. Found by a customer's kid half an hour ago. Victim was bludgeoned to death." He pointed at a four foot, three-inch diameter branch that had a yellow evidence marker next to it. "We are pretty sure that's the murder weapon."

MacFarland stared at the log. "Not likely to get prints off of that. Might be able to get DNA, though."

"Yeah, we'll see. Turn it over to Forensics, let them do their CSI magic on it."

MacFarland examined the crime scene. It was out of sight of the front gate, almost in a cul-de-sac formed by the rows of Christmas trees. People driving by the lot wouldn't see what was happening back here, nor, for that matter, would most of the customers, if any, who were in the lot at the time the murder took place.

"Got an ID on the vic yet?"

"It's Ozzie, Mac, it's Ozzie!" Leroy whispered in an anguished tone.

Lockwood shot an annoyed glance at Leroy. "Yes, it's a guy named Ozzie Smith. You know him, Mac?"

"Yes, I do, as a matter of fact. I had Thanksgiving dinner with him. You said a customer found him?"

"Yeah, a little kid, about five years old." Lockwood checked his notes. "His name is Zayne Cortland, Zayne with a 'y'. His parents are Jeffry and Linda Cortland."

"Zayne with a 'y'? What kind of name is that? Why can't parents give their kids real names anymore?"

Lockwood shook his head. "Don't know the answer to that, Mac. What I can't understand is how someone could kill Santa and no one noticed."

"What about the owner? Who's he?"

"That would be Caleb Smales. He says he came in at six this morning to open up the lot, been here ever since. When he heard the commotion, he called the police."

"I can't believe this happened," said Leroy.

"You're one of the employees here?" asked Lockwood. "Did someone take your statement?"

"He and the victim used to live together," offered MacFarland.

"Make sure you give your particulars to one of the uniformed officers," said Lockwood before he headed off towards the cluster of uniforms that were still gathered around the parking lot booth.

As Lockwood walked away, MacFarland grabbed Leroy's arm and pulled him off to one side, more out of earshot of the police.

"Leroy, did you see anything unusual yesterday or today?"

"Unusual how?"

"I guess like any confrontations between Ozzie and Caleb? Or with anyone else?"

"Well, yeah, there is this one thing, but it doesn't have anything to do with Ozzie. I mean, not really. But it does involve that kid."

"The kid? What thing?"

"I told you that Caleb checks every tree when it

comes off the truck, right? Yesterday, we get about fifty trees come in, and there is Caleb checking the trees. Then he pulls this one tree aside, and I'm thinking it's just an ordinary tree, but it isn't. It's different."

"How?"

"It has a big red 'Sold' tag on it. I'm wondering, how can the tree be sold before it even gets here, and then I think to myself, well, of course, it's because they want the tree for themself. So it musta been Caleb's brother Thomas who put the Sold tag on it. So of course, that don't concern me, and I forget all about it. Until later, that is."

"What happened then?"

"Caleb put the tree to one side, near the booth, like it was special, you know. But some kid comes in with his parents, but they're not watching him. You know, parents should watch their kids a lot more. They don't do that anymore, and these kids just run wild."

"What did the kid do, Leroy?"

"He went and pulled the red tag off the tree. Ozzie seen that and he yelled at the kid and grabbed the tag from the little monster. His parents get upset—*now* they are paying attention to him! And Caleb gets upset, but he gets upset with Ozzie, I don't know why. He grabs the red tag and puts it on one of the trees near the booth, but it's a different tree. Ozzie tries to tell him, but Caleb just yells at Ozzie and threatens to fire him, so Ozzie backs off. Ozzie is really a very peace-loving guy. He doesn't like confrontation, you know."

MacFarland returned to his hot dog stand and relayed the morning's news to Rufus. The Vietnam vet looked perturbed. "I hope Leroy don't get accused of killing Ozzie," he said.

MacFarland frowned. "If he does get charged, I'll be in his corner. But don't worry. I'm sure Leroy won't be charged with murder."

THURSDAY MORNING CYNTHIA PIERSON, MacFarland's former partner on the Denver Police force and his current landlady, notified him that the police were holding Leroy Aflack as a person of interest.

"You're kidding me, right? Leroy is no more guilty than I am."

"Not a good comparison, Mac. Don't worry. Apparently Rufus told him to contact Jerry Baker. Leroy should be back on the streets by this afternoon."

That wasn't good enough for MacFarland. He was fairly certain that Leroy would not kill his best friend, certainly not in such a brutal way. The bludgeoning had all the earmarks of an enraged assailant. MacFarland questioned whether anything would enrage Leroy.

"Of course I don't really know him that well," admitted MacFarland to Rufus.

"But I know him, boss. And you're right. Leroy wouldn't do that. He and Ozzie was even closer than us are."

"Then the only thing to do is find out who really killed Ozzie."

MacFarland strolled over to Caleb's lot, which wasn't far from the corner where he operated his hot dog stand. Rufus handled the cart, as he often did when MacFarland was poking around a case.

MarFarland posed as a customer looking for a tree. Leroy had told him that Caleb had employed four men to work his lot. Leroy, of course; Ozzie, now deceased; Juan, and Keith. MacFarland discovered that with Ozzie's death, Roxanne had been roped back into working on the lot.

He encountered her first. She wasn't dressed up like Santa or one of his elves. Instead she wore a long dress of cheap scarlet velvet trimmed by white fur as fake as her boobs. MacFarland assumed that she was supposed to be Santa's wife.

She would have looked great in the elf costume.

"What kind of tree you want, mister? Big one, little one?"

"I'm not sure. I don't have a lot of space to put a tree."

"Little one, then. We got a bunch of them over here."

MacFarland followed her over to a front section of the lot. "My name is Mark, by the way."

Roxanne gave him a look that indicated she didn't trust anyone with the name of Mark. Or perhaps it was a look that said she didn't trust any man who might be trying to make a pass at her. In any case, she didn't offer her name. "Here's the little ones."

"Ouch! Thirty bucks for that tree?"

"Trees are expensive," said Roxanne. "But as my husband says, trees are God's gift to humanity."

"You're Caleb's wife?"

"You know Caleb? Yeah, I am. Roxy. How do you know Caleb?" Roxanne's tone was cautious. Surprisingly cautious.

"I have a hot dog stand a couple of blocks over. I sometimes park here."

"Oh. I thought you was a cop. You look like a cop."

MacFarland got this fairly often. He wasn't exactly sure what it was that made people think he was still a cop, but he quickly denied it. "Nope. Just a hot dog vendor."

"How can you make a living selling hot dogs? Anyhow, you want that tree?"

"Still thinking about it. Say, I hear there was some trouble over here the other day. One of your employees got hurt?"

"Stupid ass got himself killed," said Roxanne. "Don't know what he was doing here after his shift ended anyway. Probably trying to rob us."

"How do you know he was killed after his shift?"

Roxanne was about to answer, then clammed up. "If you see any tree you like, bring it over to the office, and we can check you out." She headed back to the booth, glancing over her shoulder at him as she walked away.

MacFarland saw another employee dressed up in an elf costume just finishing up with a customer. As the employee headed towards the front of the lot, MacFarland went over to him. "Keith?"

The man looked at MacFarland in surprise. "Yeah, how can I help you?"

"Were you working here the day Ozzie was killed?"

"I was here in the afternoon, but I didn't see it. Why? Who are you?"

"Just someone who was a friend of Ozzie's, trying to find out what happened to him."

"I don't know much about what happened to him. As I said, I was gone when he must have gotten killed."

"Did you see anyone who had a problem with Ozzie?"

"A problem with him? No, not that I saw. I did see him arguing with Mr. Smales, though. I think it might have been because a customer got upset with Ozzie for what he did with their kid."

"What did he do with the kid?"

"Nothing serious. The kid was pulling tags off of the trees. We don't like that, because then we have to go re-tag them. I guess Ozzie yelled at the kid. Might have pushed him away. At any rate, whatever he did, the kid's parents got upset and started threatening to sue Caleb. They had some words and then Caleb gave it to Ozzie. I thought he was going to punch Ozzie, but he didn't."

"What happened to the parents? Did they--"

"What the hell are you doing?"

MacFarland felt a hand on his shoulder, trying to spin him around. Instinctively, he ducked and spun around, grabbing the man's arm and twisting it severely. He wasn't surprised to see that his assailant was Caleb Smales. Roxanne Smales was a few steps behind him, a wry smile on her face.

"Don't grab hold of people like that, Mr. Smales," he said. "You might get hurt."

"What are you doing, harassing my employees? I know you! You're that damn Hot Dog Detective! This is private property, you have no business being here."

"I'm just here to buy a Christmas tree, Mr. Smales. I'm sure your wife will attest to that."

Roxanne's smile disappeared. "He was looking at trees, Caleb. But he started asking strange questions."

Caleb turned towards Keith. "Was he talking to you about buying a tree?"

Keith looked quickly from Caleb to MacFarland, then nodded. "Yes sir, we were just talking about what trees shed the fewest needles."

Caleb scowled at Keith, then backed up a step. "Sorry I grabbed you," he said. He turned, grabbed Roxanne rather roughly, and dragged her back towards the booth.

"Thanks," said MacFarland to Keith.

"Don't mention it. The guy is a total asswipe."

As MacFarland headed back to his hot dog stand, he smiled. His visit to the lot hadn't been a complete waste of time. He now had two suspects in the murder of Ozzie Smith. Caleb Smales and the irate customer.

He knew where to find Caleb Smales. Now he had to find Jeffry Cortland.

CHAPTER FIVE
THURSDAY, NOVEMBER 30, 1545 HOURS

IT DIDN'T TAKE MacFarland long to track down Jeffry Cortland. With just a little bit of searching, MacFarland was able to find the Cortland's home address, work history, and even arrest record.

It helped that Benny Lockwood was willing to dig up all that information for MacFarland.

"Why do you think he's involved?" asked Lockwood.

"Oh, just a hunch."

"I've heard about the MacFarland hunches," said Lockwood thoughtfully. "So you think he was more than just a customer?"

"I do," said MacFarland, looking at the printout of Cortland's arrest record. "A couple of citations for DUI, domestic violence, and one for assault. Seems that Mr. Cortland has quite a temper."

"Maybe his son finding the body was just bad luck."

"You could say that again." He looked around the squad room. "Where's Pierson?"

Lockwood looked around. "Probably trying to clean

up her caseload. She insists she's going to take Christmas off this year."

"I'm not sure if she celebrates Christmas. She never has a tree or any decorations up."

"Really? I hadn't noticed. I usually take my vacation at Christmas time. If I can."

MacFarland got a conspiratorial glint in his eye. "You know what would be good? If we decorated her desk up with all sorts of Christmas decorations."

Lockwood looked over at Pierson's desk with doubt clouding his face. "Now that you mention it, maybe she doesn't celebrate Christmas."

It turned out that Jeffry Cortland ran a Christmas tree lot on the other side of Speer Boulevard. MacFarland drove over to Cortland's tree lot. It was about half the size of the lot Caleb Smales ran. There were two young men working the lot. MacFarland went up to the first one.

"I'm looking for Jeffry Cortland," he said.

The young man, a deep scar on the side of his face, looked around. "He must be in the truck."

MacFarland looked around for a truck, but didn't see one.

"Over there, behind the donut shop," said the scarred man.

MacFarland went over to the truck and knocked on a door. The door opened and a man peeked out. "Can I help you?"

"Are you Jeffry Cortland?"

The man nodded. "What can I do for you? Who are you?"

"My name is Mark MacFarland. I have some questions about the incident that happened a couple of days ago."

"You mean the murder of that man over on Caleb's lot? I didn't have anything to do with it."

"Your son did find the body."

"Yeah, and we're dealing with the trauma of that! Probably scarred him for life! I can just see the thousands we'll have to spend getting therapy for Zayne."

"I understand you had a run-in with the deceased the day before."

"Who told you that?"

"It seems to be something that you failed to mention to the police when they were interrogating witnesses."

"My son had just found a dead man, for God's sake! I wasn't thinking about what might have happened earlier."

"As I understand it, Mr. Cortland, you threatened to sue Mr. Smales over whatever might have happened. How about you tell me what did occur between the victim, your son, you, and Mr. Smales?"

"I tell you, nothing happened. Okay, I'll tell you what happened, but it's not relevant to that man's death."

"Go on, I'm waiting."

"The man wearing the Santa costume was yelling at my son. My wife and I heard him yelling, and at first we didn't think anything of it. Then I see him shove my boy, almost knocking him down! I don't know about you, but when a grown man beats up a small child, my blood boils! I went over to put a stop to it..."

"Wait, are you saying that the Santa kept going after your boy?"

"He didn't have time to. I got in his face and started telling him what I was going to do to the bastard."

"You threatened him?"

"No, I was defending my boy. Then that asshole Smales comes over and wants to know what the commotion is. The Santa guy says that my boy was ripping tags off of the trees, and he holds up a red tag to prove it. Then Smales starts yelling and cussing, telling me and my boy to get off his property. That's when I threatened to sue him. I tell you, Mister, Smales is a total jackass!"

"So if this happened on Monday, why were you back there on Tuesday? With your son, no less!"

"I—I...okay, I went back because I wasn't finished."

"You weren't finished with teaching 'that bastard' a lesson?"

"You mean the Santa? Hell no, I didn't kill him. I went back to find out how much Caleb was charging for different trees. The Christmas tree business is a cutthroat business Mr. MacFarland. Cutthroat, I tell you."

LEROY STOPPED by MacFarland's hot dog cart on Friday morning, with the news that his lawyer, Jerry Baker—"the best lawyer in the world!"—had gotten him released right away. MacFarland didn't feel a need to say that Leroy could have gotten himself released simply by asking if he was being charged or arrested. If not, then he would have been free to go. But it was better to have a lawyer involved.

MacFarland couldn't believe that he even had that thought. When he was a cop, lawyers were his bane.

MacFarland hadn't had any luck proving the irate parents had anything to do with the murder. He had intended to ask Leroy if he knew anything about the couple, but the press of customers on Friday morning made it difficult to conduct any detective business. He vowed that he would try to talk to Leroy at the end of the day.

MacFarland and Rufus were shutting down the hot dog cart when Leroy hurried up to the cart.

"I'm glad I caught you before you left," he said. "I wanted to tell you what happened."

"What happened?" asked Rufus.

Leroy gloated. "I got even with Caleb!" He laughed. "I never knew that the best part of working was getting even with your boss."

"We used to do that with Second Lieutenants," said MacFarland. "Always thought they were the most conceited people in the army."

MacFarland gave Rufus an annoyed scowl. "Not nice, Rufus. What did you do, Leroy?"

"I told you about those red tags that come in already on the trees? I used to think that they were trees that Caleb or his brother wanted to keep for themselves, mostly because they were really nice trees. But another red tagged tree came in today, so I got to wondering, how many trees are they getting for themselves?"

"I thought some of the red tags came off. Maybe they never got the trees they saved."

"Maybe."

"Or maybe," suggested Rufus, "their family is really huge and they needs lots of trees."

"Maybe that too. Never thought of that."

"I don't see anything wrong with picking out the best tree for yourself," said MacFarland. "It just sounds like one of the perks of selling Christmas trees."

"I don't know about perks, but I do know about jerks, and Caleb Smales is one big jerk."

MacFarland couldn't help smiling, since he felt the same way. "So what did you do, Leroy?"

"I waited until Caleb wasn't around, and then I

changed the red tag from the tree he put aside to another one that looked almost the same. So in a sense, he's still getting a nice tree. I couldn't see the difference. Then I put that tree aside." Leroy smiled broadly. "I think I am going to buy the tree for our new house."

"That's a great idea, Leroy," said Rufus.

MacFarland frowned. "Are you sure that Caleb didn't see you make the switch?"

"Positive! He and that grumpy wife of his were busy arguing in the booth. I know he didn't see me."

"I'm not sure I can condone what you did, Leroy. It is, in a manner of speaking, stealing."

Leroy waved his hand, brushing off MacFarland's comment. "Naw, it's not stealing. If you want to know what stealing is, it's what he charges for those trees. There wasn't a price on the one I put aside, but trees like that sell for a hundred bucks!"

"I ain't bought any Christmas trees since I was a kid, and it wasn't me who bought them then, so I don't know how much to pay."

"I'm in the same boat, Rufus. They do strike me as being pretty expensive. Maybe that's why Pierson doesn't have Christmas trees. She's not the Grinch...she's Scrooge."

"Boss, you're gonna get into trouble if you keep saying things like that about the lady cop."

MacFarland smiled. "I'm only joking, Rufus. You know that."

"Yeah, but when I tell her what you say, she doesn't think it's a joke."

"What? You tell her what I say?"

Rufus looked sheepish. "Not all the time. Just when she asks me how my day was. Since my day is dull as cow dung, I tell her what happened to you. And if nothing happened, I tell her what you say."

"From now on, what I say to you stays with you, got it?"

"Sort of like Las Vegas, right?"

"Right. Now, as for your tree, Leroy, how about this. I will come by tomorrow and buy the tree for your household. That way you can save up your money, and you won't risk Caleb recognizing the tree as the one he wanted."

"You'd do that for us? Hell, man, that's really nice of you."

"The boss may not have much, Leroy, but he does got the Christmas spirit."

MACFARLAND KNEW that he would not get much help from Rufus this day. April Evans had come by, not in her capacity as a Denver health inspector, but as Rufus' main squeeze, a role enthusiastically supported by both April and Rufus. *When had their relationship gotten so serious?* wondered MacFarland.

He couldn't really complain. April's presence actually seemed to help attract customers. The frequent laughter, the jovial atmosphere that she brought with her, all seemed to attract customers to MacFarland's corner and his hot dog stand. Despite the cold, laughter seemed to warm up the day.

It was the mid-morning lull when Leroy came over to the MacFarland's hot dog cart. He bought a cup of coffee and a bratwurst, which he ate while talking to Rufus and April. He began to tell them about the mysterious red tags.

"Every couple of days, we get these shipments of trees in. Sometimes one of the trees will have a red Sold tag on it, but most of the time the trees don't have any tags. No, that's not true. They have a tag with the type of tree on it. You know, Douglas Fir, Canine Fir, you know all those types. But not Red tags. And they don't have prices on them. We have to put the price tags on the trees."

"Who are the trees sold to?"

"I don't know," admitted Leroy. "I used to think that they were sold to Caleb or his family, but now I'm not so sure. I don't ever remember seeing him take any of those trees home. No, wait. There is one guy who seemed interested in one of the trees. He took a Red tag tree. It must not have been okay, because he came back the next day really angry. Caleb and he had a big argument, and then the customer stomped off."

"Maybe Caleb doesn't know how to provide good customer service. Pleasing customers is the first rule of being a good business person, right, April?"

"It sure is, honey, and you do a good job of pleasing your customers!"

MacFarland rolled his eyes. "Keep it G-rated, you two," he advised.

"You know, you guys should check it out!" said Leroy.

"Check out what?" asked Rufus.

"The red tag mystery."

"It doesn't sound like there's much of a mystery there," said April.

"No, really, there is. Now, here's the mystery. Why is there only one tree with a red tag every shipment?"

"I thought you said that it wasn't every shipment?"

"It isn't every shipment, so maybe it's a red tag in

every couple of shipments. Yeah, that's a better way to say it."

"Maybe the owner is picking out trees for his friends. I still don't see a mystery, Leroy."

"Okay, why does the same guy keep coming by?"

"What same guy? You didn't say nothing about some same guy. If you want a good mystery, you got to get your facts straight."

"The guy that came in for the red tag tree. He came back the next day, all angry. I did tell you about him. I got my facts straight."

"Oh, that don't mean nothing," said Rufus, scratching his beard. "He was just an upset customer."

"Then why's he been back again?"

"Are you sure it's the same guy?" asked MacFarland, simultaneously kicking himself for encouraging them.

Leroy nodded. "No mistaking this dude. Big as a mountain, red hair and red beard. Did I say he was big? Yeah, like he's a tackle on a football team or something. And mean-looking. I wouldn't want this guy angry with me. No, there's no mistaking him."

MacFarland frowned. He did recall seeing a tall, muscular red-head over at the tree lot at least once in the past week. He couldn't remember exactly where the man was, but despite wearing a heavy coat and a hat, there was no mistaking "a mountain of a man."

"I wonder if the big red man is a relative," he suggested.

"He sure don't look like Caleb or Thomas, his brother. I don't think he's their brother."

"There are other relationships besides brothers," said April, smiling.

"Oh. Yeah, guess so. Didn't think of that. But what do you say? Is there a mystery there or not? I mean, look, one person has already been killed because of these red tags."

"What do you want us to do?" asked April.

"I don't know. Detective work."

"That's what the boss does," said Rufus. "We're not detectives. We just run a hot dog cart. Oh, and inspect things."

"Yeah, I don't think this is such a good idea, Leroy. As you said, one person has already been killed, though we have no evidence that Ozzie's death had anything to do with those red tags. The police think it was a robbery gone bad."

"What about our mystery?"

MacFarland shook his head. "Leroy, if there really is a mystery there, which I don't believe for one moment, my advice is to let the police handle it. You don't have the training to get involved in this type of thing. Focus on your job, enjoy the holidays. Listen, after work, I'll come by and pick up that tree you put aside. But only on one condition."

"What's that?"

"That you drop this detective crap. Leave it to the professionals."

Leroy, Rufus, and April all looked at each other. Finally, Leroy nodded. "Okay, I guess we'll drop it."

As Leroy headed off to the Christmas tree lot, MacFarland had a sinking feeling that none of the three conspirators planned on dropping their crazy idea.

JUST AFTER LUNCHTIME, Rufus and April wandered off. MacFarland could not tell if they went to retrieve April's car or if they continued on to the next parking lot where the Christmas tree murder had taken place. He hoped that they had the good sense to go to April's house and do whatever romantically involved couples do when they have free time and privacy.

When it came time to shut down his cart, MacFarland found that he had been abandoned. Rufus hadn't returned from his afternoon tryst. Grumbling, MacFarland closed up his cart, locked the cash drawer, and headed over to get his truck. It had been a long time since he had to do this without Rufus' help, and he realized with a start that he had come to depend on Rufus. As someone who usually regarded himself as a loner, it was disconcerting to realize that he was not nearly as independent as he thought.

He got his truck positioned and connected his hot dog

stand to the hitch. It was only then that he remembered he promised to pick up the Christmas tree this evening. He should have done that before he hooked up his stand. Cursing his lack of planning, he drove around the block and down to Thirteenth. He took Thirteenth to Speer, then up to Galapago. He was able to park his truck, albeit illegally, near the entrance to the Christmas tree lot. He got out and headed into the lot. He spied Leroy, assembling wooden stands to a new supply of trees. Waving, he went over to Leroy.

"Where's that tree you were holding for me?" he asked.

Leroy, concentrating on what he was doing, looked up in surprise. "Oh, right. Yeah, it's over there. Come on, I'll get it for you."

As they headed across the lot, MacFarland checked who else was working this evening. He recognized Keith and Juan, then stopped. On the far side of the lot, past the booth, two men were engaged in an animated, if given the distance, silent discussion. One of the men, the one with his back to MacFarland, was nonetheless easy to identify. It was Caleb Smales.

It was the other man who caught MacFarland's attention.

He was a big man, easily six feet eight inches in height. His bulk was evident, even though he was wearing a heavy parka.

But what was most noticeable about the man was his red hair and beard.

The red-headed man certainly was around the Christmas tree lot a lot. Maybe he was a relative and simply disagreed with the high prices Caleb was charging for the trees.

"This is the tree," said Leroy. "Looks pretty much like any other tree. Maybe a little fuller than most, but that's about it."

"How much is it?" asked MacFarland.

Leroy looked at the price, then smiled sheepishly. "One hundred twenty dollars."

"Ouch! You guys are crooks!"

"I don't set the prices. I just put them on the trees. What's really upsetting, Mac, is that I only get one dollar for selling this tree. Same as I would get for selling our cheapest tree. That doesn't seem fair to me."

"In a strange way, it does make some sense," said MacFarland, paying for the tree and pocketing the receipt. "You get incentivized to sell as many trees as you can, not just the most expensive. As a matter of fact, you get more if you sell the smaller, cheaper trees."

"How does that help the business?"

"I bet Caleb pays the same for each tree when he buys it from the tree farm, so moving the most number of trees is where he makes money. But I could be wrong. I don't know the Christmas tree business. Let me take the tree to my truck before I get a ticket."

MacFarland grabbed hold of the tree and started towards his truck. He was near the entrance when he saw that Caleb Smales was blocking his path.

"You can't have that tree," said Caleb.

"I just bought it," said MacFarland. He pulled the receipt out of his pocket and waved it. "It says right here on the receipt, 'All sales final.' I think that means I own this tree."

"You weren't supposed to buy that one. I recognize it. It was intended for some other customer."

"Really? I didn't see any sign on the tree, no paid receipt. Would you please move out of my way? I have to get home."

"No, you can't take that tree!"

Caleb tried to grab the tree, but MacFarland grabbed hold of Caleb's hand and bent his fingers back. Caleb dropped to his knees, twisting himself around to avoid having his hand broken. MacFarland released Caleb's fingers and headed towards his truck.

"Rufus is right," he muttered to himself. "The guy just doesn't know how to provide good customer service."

MACFARLAND HAD JUST UNHOOKED his cart from his truck when Rufus came bouncing out of the house. "Boss, good thing you got home! What took you so long, we expected you an hour ago."

MacFarland didn't answer, but continued disconnecting the electrical leads from his truck to the cart. "I had errands to do," he finally said.

Rufus helped push the hot dog stand into its storage space. "Well, you got to clean up cause we're about to leave."

"What are you babbling about, Rufus?"

"We're going to see the Parade of Lights. We're gonna go in the Lady Cop's car cause she can get parking easier than we can."

MacFarland frowned. Pierson was going to misuse her police vehicle privileges? Didn't sound like her. "Let me get that tree out of the bed," he said. When had he agreed to go see the Parade of Lights? Didn't Rufus know how much he disliked crowds? You never knew how many pickpockets and thieves were hiding in the crowd. He took the time to knock the wooden brace off of the base of the tree and put the tree into a bucket of water. He left the tree in the garage where it would be protected from excessive cold during the night.

Pierson came out of the house, followed by April. "Took you long enough," she laughed. "Hop in my car, we're going to party tonight."

Pierson's copper hair caught the light from the back porch, haloing her head. She had a dimpled chin, a sensual jaw, and full pouty lips that for once were smiling happily. In Pierson's line of work, there were few reasons to smile, and MacFarland appreciated her smile whenever he saw it.

MacFarland climbed into the front passenger seat and examined Pierson closely. "Who are you and what have you done with my former partner?"

Pierson smiled again. "Mac, it's the holiday season. Lighten up and enjoy yourself."

MacFarland turned around and looked at Rufus and April sitting in the back seat, shyly holding hands. "Are we on a double-date?"

Pierson laughed. "Not exactly. They're on a date, we're just going to chaperone them."

"When did we decide to go to Parade of Lights?" asked MacFarland.

Pierson shot him a glance. "Last week. We said we were going to make this a special holiday season for all of us."

"Oh. We did? I thought you didn't like Christmas."

Pierson frowned. "Where'd you get that idea?"

"I've never seen you put up a tree or lights or anything. I thought you had some tragic memories associated with Christmas."

Pierson shook her head, laughing. "Do you know how many burglaries occur around Christmas? How many spouses decide to give their better half a bullet for the holidays? I'm always working during the holidays!"

"It's work? Not because you're a Scrooge?"

"Where do you come up with these things? I have a whole closet full of Christmas decorations I'm never able to use because I make it possible for cops with families to have some time off. Mary, Mother of God, give me patience!"

When they arrived downtown, Pierson didn't use her position as a member of the police force to get a good parking space. In fact, they parked quite a ways from the parade route.

"How far are we from the parade?" asked Rufus.

"Only a few blocks," said MacFarland. He didn't add that they were a few long blocks. "You should have used your cop status to get us closer."

"I don't believe in abusing my position," said Pierson.

The four of them found a place to watch the parade on the 17th Street Mall, along with thousands of other revelers. The mood of the crowd was jovial, despite a later start than usual. MacFarland and Rufus battled a crowd at a coffee shop to purchase four eggnog lattes for everyone. They arrived back at their spot just as the first marching band passed by.

"Good thing they got them lights on them," observed

Rufus. "Otherwise, with them dark uniforms, we might miss them."

"Oh, Rufus, you are such a card!" gushed April.

"Hey, here comes Major Waddles!" said Rufus. "He's my favorite. I usta watch him before he even had a name."

"I didn't realize you watched the Parade of Lights, Rufus."

"There's a lot I usta do before you were on the streets, boss. Ever since I met you, though, my social life dried up."

"I'm sorry to hear that."

"Oh, it's no big deal. When you're homeless, you don't have much of a social life anyway. I didn't really lose out on very much. Except, maybe, for the Parade of Lights."

"We'll try to change that from now on, Rufus."

"We sure will," added April.

"I should have worn my heavy coat," said Pierson. "It's a lot colder out here than I thought it would be. How did you guys survive the winter?"

"I usta have my hidey-hole. It was warm and toasty."

MacFarland shook his head. "His hidey-hole," he explained to April, "was a large unused storm drain pipe that emptied into the Platte River. It was hardly warm and toasty."

"I'm glad you're not homeless now," said April.

MacFarland wrapped his arms around Pierson. Surprisingly, she didn't object, but snuggled into his arms. "It was rough when we were living on the streets.

But as I've always said, some good can come out of any bad thing."

Pierson looked up at him, amusement softening her face. "You always say that?"

"Sure. If I hadn't been homeless I wouldn't have met Rufus, which means I wouldn't have met Leroy, I wouldn't have met Ozzie, which means no one would be trying to figure out what happened to Ozzie to get him some justice."

"I thought we was going to leave that to the professionals, boss," said Rufus.

"Of course we are. What I meant to say is, now I can get a tree for Gracie and Kirk."

Rufus snuggled closer to April. "See, I told you, boss has the Christmas spirit. Hey, there's Santa!"

CHAPTER TEN

MACFARLAND WAS in a good mood most of Sunday. Even though the temporary intimacy with Pierson, which he had to admit had to do more with abating freezing temperatures than rising passionate heat, did not last the evening, he still found it enjoyable merely being close to her.

It wasn't until he was shivering in a stiff morning breeze that he finally admitted to himself that Pierson was simply being friendly for the holidays. What had passed between them Saturday night was nothing more than the good feelings sparked by the season of the year. Or possibly the prospect of having time off this Christmas.

"You know, I should have kept that tree for us," said MacFarland.

"I thought you got it for Kirk and Gracie and the others. You left it on their porch."

"I did. But if Pierson is going to take time off this

Christmas, maybe we should have our own tree. She said she has decorations."

"I wonder what kind of decorations Kirk and Gracie have. I'm not even sure they have furniture."

"I did leave a tree stand for them to use. I didn't think they'd have one of those, and you can't stand it up in a bucket like I did in the garage."

"You think of everything, boss."

"Not everything, Rufus. Which reminds me, why aren't you with April?"

"She's with her sister, shopping for Christmas."

"I didn't know she had a sister."

"Yeah, she's a twin. Can you believe it? There are two beautiful women in the world!"

MacFarland smiled. "Good thing for you that you don't have to choose between them."

Rufus allowed himself a rare guffaw. "I never thought of that. But I wouldn't have to choose anyway, because Liz is already married. She's got a boatload of kids. April is gonna invite me to her sister's house for Christmas."

"You mean you won't spend it with me and Cyn?"

"I didn't say that. I said that her sister has a bunch of kids. The only thing worse than an army of Viet Cong is a bunch of kids. I think I will only survive a couple of hours there."

"Good thing you have your basement hidey-hole."

"Yeah. So you think we might celebrate Christmas at the lady cop's house?"

"I'm thinking that is more and more likely, Rufus."

"Then we better get a tree."

MacFarland nodded. "Tell you what. When we shut down the cart tonight, we'll go over to Caleb's tree lot and buy a tree. It shouldn't be hard to carry it back to the truck, then pick up the cart."

"Sounds like a plan, boss. Except for one thing. Didn't you say that you sort of pissed off Caleb yesterday?"

"It was just a stupid dispute over which tree I bought. As far as I can tell, they all look alike. The guy has hundreds just like it. I'm sure he's forgotten all about it by now."

At six o'clock, after shutting down the hot dog cart, MacFarland and Rufus walked over to Caleb's parking lot. They were checking out trees when MacFarland tapped Rufus on the shoulder and pointed to a back corner of the lot. "Rufus, what is that guy doing?"

Rufus looked in the direction MacFarland pointed. "Damn, boss, it looks like he's trying to start a fire. I think he's trying to burn down the trees!"

That was exactly what MacFarland thought as he sprinted towards the arsonist. He tackled the man, knocking a cigarette lighter from the man's hand. A gasoline can crashed onto the ground, spilling a wide puddle.

"Rufus, have them call the police!" yelled MacFarland. The man he tackled was thrashing about, trying to wrestle MacFarland off of him. For his part, MacFarland fended off the man's punches, finally pinning one of the man's arms with his body. Then MacFarland heard the sound of people running towards him. Several pairs of arms grabbed hold of the arsonist as well as MacFarland, pulling them apart. MacFarland allowed himself to be pulled up. He looked around, seeing Rufus, Leroy, and several police officers.

Once MacFarland and the arsonist had some separation between them, MacFarland stared at the young man in surprise. He had a deep scar on the side of his face.

"He's the one who was trying to start the fire," said Rufus, pointing at the scarred man. "My friend just tried to stop him."

One of the uniformed officers looked at MacFarland. "MacFarland? Is that you?"

MacFarland nodded. "I was able to knock the cigarette lighter from his hand. It should be over there on the ground. Be careful, it smells like he spilled gasoline all over the place."

One of the uniformed officers called the fire department. At that moment, Caleb ran up to the group, quickly trying to understand what was happening. When he saw the arsonist, he must have recognized him as someone who worked for his competitor. He started yelling, "He's the one who killed my employee! I'm positive, he's the one!"

The young man looked surprised, and was still protesting his innocence as the police dragged him off.

MacFarland and Rufus gave a quick statement to one of the officers, then slowly headed back to pick up MacFarland's truck.

"Hey, you know, boss, we forgot to get a tree. But at least we caught a killer! Pretty good work for one night."

MacFarland shook his head. "No, Rufus. I don't

think that man was the killer. Yeah, he might be helping his boss put Caleb out of business, but I don't think he killed Ozzie Smith. But I'm pretty sure I know who did kill Ozzie."

ALTHOUGH MACFARLAND and Rufus had shut down their cart, there were enough people milling around the intersection of Fourteenth and Elati that MacFarland opened it up again. The rollers took too long to heat up, but the microwave worked like a charm to reheat hot dogs and brats that had already been cooked.

After handling the small crowd surge, and passing out the remnants of their product to some homeless people who meandered by, MacFarland and Rufus shut down their cart for the second time. They hooked the hot dog stand up to the truck and pulled out into traffic.

"Hey, boss, you know, since we saved that guy's whole flock of trees, maybe he might give us one as a reward."

"Caleb Smales does not seem like the kind of guy who expresses gratitude, Rufus."

"You never know until you ask."

MacFarland shrugged, then drove over to Caleb's tree lot. MacFarland pulled into a couple of empty parking spaces and turned off his engine. He stared at the Christmas tree lot in dismay. The lights were out and the gate was closed. As he and Rufus sat there wondering what to do next, they saw Leroy walking home.

MacFarland was about to offer Leroy a ride home when he observed Caleb get into his car and slowly follow Leroy. At first he wasn't sure Caleb really was following Leroy, but when Caleb pulled into a parking space, waited for Leroy to get a block further, and then slowly pulled out again, MacFarland was certain. After a few minutes, Leroy and Caleb were out of sight.

MacFarland and Rufus looked at each other.

"Wonder what that's about?" said Rufus.

"I don't know, but whatever it is, I don't like it."

"Me either, boss. Let's follow him."

MacFarland frowned. "Rufus, we're in a Ford F350 pulling a hot dog cart. Don't you think we'd be rather obvious?"

"Yeah, you're right. Then what can we do?"

"We know where Leroy lives. Let's go there, park a block over and wait for Leroy to get home. If Caleb is following Leroy, we should be able to catch him at Leroy's house."

"Can I borrow your phone, boss?"

Surprised, MacFarland pulled out his phone and handed it to Rufus. Rufus rarely made calls. "Oh, good idea. Call up Kirk and Gracie and warn them."

"Oh, I wasn't going to call them. I was going to call April and tell her where we're going. We was supposed to meet tonight, but it's getting kinda late."

"Hmmm. I still think you should call Kirk and Gracie

and warn them."

"Do you know their number?"

"No, I don't. I've never had reason to call them. I guess we stick to our original plan."

"Nothing better than an original plan," said Rufus, punching in the numbers to April's cell phone.

MacFarland had problems finding a place to park his truck and hot dog stand in the residential neighborhood where the homeless people had their house. He finally found a place where he could park, but it was further away than he expected. "I hope we're not too late."

They hurried over to the house, then moved more cautiously up the front walk to the porch. The front door was open a bit, and MacFarland could hear several people talking inside the house.

"I'll give you a hundred dollars for the tree," he heard Caleb say. Caleb's voice was muffled, as though he had his back to the front door.

"It's not for sale," said Gracie.

"It's our Christmas tree," said Leroy. "Our first Christmas tree."

"You damn fools, you don't even have decorations! It looks like you've got it covered with garbage!"

"That's not garbage!" yelled Gloria. "Those are strings of popcorn and popcorn ball ornaments! Hey, someone took a bite out of that ornament!"

"I want that tree."

"I'm sorry, Mr. Smales, but you can't have it. That tree was a present from our friend. Now, if you'll just leave..."

"Get your hands off of me, damn you Leroy!"

MacFarland could hear a struggle, so he pushed open the door and raced inside. He could see Leroy and Caleb wrestling with each other. Kirk, Gracie, and Gloria stood on the far side of the room, mouths opened in surprise. Harry was frozen on the opposite side of the room, holding a rolling pin.

MacFarland pulled Caleb away from Leroy, mainly to stop the fight, but Caleb wasn't prepared to stop. He began punching MacFarland, who suddenly found himself backing away from the outraged man. As Caleb swung a roundhouse punch at MacFarland, MacFarland stepped in, landing several quick jabs to Caleb's face. Caleb screamed, then leaped onto MacFarland, knocking both of them to the floor. MacFarland and Caleb grappled with each other, standing once more and twisting each other to gain an advantage.

MacFarland thought he had gained that advantage when he suddenly felt a crashing blow to the back of his head. He crumbled to the ground, his vision blurred and his head feeling like it was about to explode. When everything in front of him finally came back into focus, he saw Smales standing a few feet from him, a gun in the man's hands, the barrel pointed right at MacFarland.

"Get back, all of you! I swear I will shoot him if you don't move immediately! You, you asshole! Drop that damn rolling pin!"

Harry, shocked at having hit MacFarland instead of Caleb, dropped the rolling pin and backed fearfully towards the others.

As Rufus and Harry joined Kirk, Gracie and Gloria in the far corner, Caleb glared at MacFarland. "You! I should have known it was you! Why are you always butting into my business? What's wrong with you? What is wrong with all of you people?"

"WHAT'S SO important about that tree?" asked MacFarland.

"It's got sentimental value," snarled Caleb. "Now, move over there with the others." He waved the gun in the direction he wanted MacFarland to move.

MacFarland shuffled slowly to where Caleb indicated. It was at that moment that there was a knock on the door, which was still wide open to the cold night air.

"Why is your door open?" asked April Evans as she walked into the house. Then she saw Caleb Smales, waving the gun around. April screamed, causing Caleb to turn around and pull the trigger.

What happened next occurred so swiftly that not even MacFarland was sure what transpired. As Caleb turned, MacFarland jumped towards the man, trying to tackle him. At the same time, Rufus ran over to protect April. Gloria started screaming at the sound of the shot. Kirk, a murderous rage in his eyes, pushed Gracie behind him and lumbered towards Caleb. Harry grabbed the rolling pin and tried to find another skull to smash. Leroy stood frozen, a shocked look on his face.

MacFarland and Caleb rolled on the ground. Another shot rang out. Damn! This was getting danger-ous! He focused all of his efforts on banging Caleb's gun hand against the floor. He knocked the gun out of Caleb's hand, then began pummeling the man's face with his fist. He only stopped when he felt Caleb go limp.

He got quickly to his feet, retrieved the gun, and pointed it at Caleb.

"Get up, Smales," he ordered.

Caleb pulled himself into a sitting position, blood dripping down his face.

MacFarland looked over towards Rufus and April. She didn't appear to be hurt. The first shot also must have gone wild. He looked around the room. Kirk was ready to pounce on Caleb. Harry stood crouched over, the rolling pin ready for action. Gracie had her arms wrapped around Gloria, trying to calm the woman's sobs.

MacFarland smiled. "Well, that turned out better than I expected." He pulled out his phone and called Pierson. He explained where he was and suggested she get over to the homeless house as quickly as she could.

He was about to disconnect his phone when he heard a gasp, and then someone said, "Drop the gun, asshole! Drop it or I kill her!"

MACFARLAND TURNED to face the door. A man had grabbed hold of April, a gun pointed at her head. He must have pushed Rufus aside, for the Vietnam vet was now sitting on the floor, looking furious and ashamed. "Drop it, now, or I will shoot her!"

MacFarland considered his options, but realized that none of them were good. He dropped the gun on the floor and took a step back. "Who are you?" he demanded.

"That's Thomas Smales," said Leroy. "He's Caleb's brother."

"You can't kill all of us," said MacFarland. "The police are on their way here right now."

"I don't want to kill anyone," snarled Thomas. "I just want to get my brother and get the fuck out of here."

Caleb stood up, retrieving his gun from the floor. He glared angrily at MacFarland as he wiped blood from his nose. "We can't just leave them, Thomas. They know too much!"

"We don't know anything," said Leroy.

"I'm not a killer," insisted Thomas. "There's got to be another way. We can't just kill eight people, Caleb."

"What way is there? They've all seen our faces. They can identify us."

"You numbskull! The cops will figure out it was us."

"That's right, Caleb. The cops will figure it all out, and they will come for you. So far, the only one you've killed is Ozzie. Don't make it worse for yourself."

"I didn't kill Ozzie!" shouted Caleb. "Neither of us did!" He waved his gun at MacFarland. "You! You're the one I really should kill!"

"You're not killing anyone," bellowed someone from the door. MacFarland looked over, hoping that it was the police.

It wasn't.

The person at the door, also brandishing a gun, was an enormous red-headed man with a rather nicely trimmed beard. He pushed his way into the room, grabbing Thomas' gun from his hand and twisting it away from the smaller man. The red-haired man put the gun in his waist band, then pushed Thomas over towards Caleb.

April, now free from Thomas' grip, scurried over towards Rufus and crouched down with him.

"Where's my money?" demanded the red-haired man. "You said you were going to get it. Where the fuck is it?"

"It's not here, Big Red," said Caleb. "We don't have it."

"Wrong answer, you dumbass!" A shot exploded and Caleb, a shocked look on his face, fell back with a frightening large hole in his chest.

"My God, you killed him! You killed my brother!"

"Shut up or you'll be next! I'm getting sick and tired of all the trouble you two have caused me. Listen, you little turd, I've already killed two people to get that money. A third won't bother me one bit."

"You killed Ozzie, didn't you?" said MacFarland.

The big red man looked at MacFarland. "The black kid? Yeah, I killed him. He got in my way."

"What's this money you keep asking about?"

"What's it to you?"

MacFarland shrugged. "I suspect you're going to kill all of us anyway. I can tell that you aren't nearly as squeamish as those two were. So, if I'm going to die, I'd at least like to know why."

The red-haired man smiled. "Damn, you got guts. I like you. I'll kill you last. Sure, I'll satisfy your curiosity. These assholes distribute drugs for me. They do that very well. What they don't do so well is pay me the money they owe me. They was supposed to pay me a hundred grand, but they lost it."

"We didn't lose it. Sharon stole it."

"I don't give a fuck what happened on your end, you jerk! You're supposed to pay me!"

"We tried!" said Thomas in a pleading voice.

"Fuck you! The only reason you're not dead yet is I need you to get me the money." The red-haired man turned back towards MacFarland, but at that moment, everyone in the room heard the screech of police sirens tearing up the street. The red-haired man got an expression of annoyance on his face and glanced back towards the front door to see whether any police vehicles were nearby.

The second or two that it took Big Red to look towards the door was all MacFarland needed. He dropped his phone on the floor and dived towards the big man's knees, trying his best to kick at Big Red's knee caps. Surprisingly, at the same time, Harry raced forward with the rolling pin. This time, aiming at a bigger target, he was more effective in hitting the right skull. As MacFarland and Harry both sprang into action, so also did Rufus, Leroy, and Kirk. Kirk body slammed into Big Red's back just as MacFarland crashed into his knees and Harry smashed the rolling pin against his head. Big Red crashed to the floor. MacFarland hopped to his feet and stomped on Big Red's gun hand. The mountainous man roared in anger, but the gun slipped out. MacFarland grasped the gun and aimed it at Big Red.

"Go on, you dirt bag! Make my day!"

Rufus glanced at MacFarland, a look of bemused surprise on his face.

MacFarland smiled back. "I've always wanted to say that. Would you believe this is the first real opportunity I've had to say it?"

The sound of sirens reached ear-splitting levels, then stopped as the police vehicles pulled up to the front of the house. A dozen uniforms, quickly followed by Pierson, raced into the house. As the police pointed their guns at everyone in the room, MacFarland, slowly putting his gun on the floor, then raising his hands. Pierson quickly assessed the situation, went over and picked up the gun.

"He's one of the good guys," she told the uniforms. She spotted his phone on the floor. She bent over and picked it up. "Pretty smart of you to leave your phone connection open, Mac. I heard everything. Not only me, I broadcast it over the police channel. I think we have the whole conversation recorded."

MacFarland stared at his phone in surprise. "I left my phone on? Oh, yeah, yeah, it was a smart thing to do."

"IT'S SO nice of you to come over," said Gracie. "Merry Christmas!"

"Thanks," said MacFarland as he and Rufus came in out of the heavy snow flurries. "Merry Christmas to you too!"

"Where's Detective Pierson?" asked Gracie.

"Would you know it? She got called in to work. She sends her apologies for missing Christmas with you guys. I guess she's not Scrooge or the Grinch. She's just dedicated." He smiled. When he learned that Pierson would have to work over the holidays, he and Lockwood had bedazzled her desk with Christmas decorations. She had called him up and thanked him for the holiday gesture.

"Hi Mac, hi Rufus," said Leroy. "Glad you could make it. Great weather today!"

"It is a white Christmas, isn't it?" Rufus shook the snow off of his jacket. "I'm supposed to go over to April's sister's house, but that's later. Besides, she's got kids, and I don't do so good around kids."

MacFarland laughed. "That's not what my niece and nephew think, Rufus! They think you're wonderful."

"Oh, really? Maybe it won't be so bad then."

MacFarland handed Kirk a large plastic bag. "We brought some presents for you and the others," he said.

"I'll put them under the tree," said Kirk, a major feat of oration for the taciturn man.

Harry came over and took MacFarland's hand. "I never got a chance to apologize for hitting you on the head."

MacFarland smiled, rubbing the back of his head. "I completely forgot about it. But you came through in the end, Harry."

Harry beamed. "Yes, I guess I did. That's the first time I've ever been heroic."

"Nonsense," said MacFarland. "It's heroic to survive on the streets and not lose hope."

"I do have one question, Mac," said Harry. "How did you know it was Big Red who killed Ozzie?"

MacFarland nodded. "I was pretty sure something was going on at the Christmas tree lot. When I heard that Big Red had been there several times, I knew he was looking for something. When Leroy here switched tags, he was pretty sure that Caleb didn't see him, but I'm pretty sure Big Red did see him do it. When I bought the tree, they panicked."

"Oh my God, I told Caleb that you gave us the tree!" said Leroy.

MacFarland nodded. "So he followed you home. The rest is history."

Gloria came out with a tray of glasses containing

eggnog. "It's not spiked," she whispered to MacFarland. "So it's okay if you drink some."

Gracie called everyone to gather around the Christmas tree. "Now that Mac's brought some more presents, we should open them up," she announced. She pointed to pillows and blankets that were spread around the room. "Sorry we don't have any furniture yet. There was a delay in getting it delivered to us."

"The floor is fine," said Leroy.

MacFarland and Rufus agreed, then found positions where they could awkwardly sit and watch the proceedings.

"Interesting tree," said Rufus.

The Christmas tree was decorated with strings of popcorn and cranberries, colored popcorn balls, and a wild assortment of strange ornaments. Some of the ornaments were origami figures, others were items you might find dumpster-diving. Shiny pieces of glass, suspended by thin copper wire; discarded computer disks; broken bric-a-brac, children's toys. MacFarland knew that in some neighborhoods, you could find pretty interesting stuff. After all, he had spent several years doing some quality dumpster-diving.

"Is that a sock?" asked Rufus.

Gracie blushed. "Yes, it's Ozzie's sock. We wanted him to have something on the tree, something personal. I suppose we should have washed the sock before we put it on the tree."

Besides the five presents MacFarland and Rufus had brought with them, there was an assortment of other presents under the tree. The five members of the household had played Secret Santa to give each other presents. Given how little money each of them had, MacFarland could easily imagine what a challenge purchasing any kind of a present was for each of them. After all, only Leroy had a job, and that had ended three weeks earlier.

Gracie sat near the tree and began to pull out presents, reading off the name of the person each present was for.

"This is for Gloria," she said. It was one of MacFarland's gifts.

Gloria opened the box, then proudly held up a pullover sweater. "Thank you, Mac."

Kirk got a woolen cap from his Secret Santa. Harry got a pair of socks that didn't look like they came from Goodwill. Gracie got a scarf and mittens (from Rufus). Leroy got a pair of boots (from MacFarland) and then a coffee cup with Leroy glazed on its side. Gloria got a set of underwear from her Secret Santa ("It's alright, Gloria, I got them for you," said Gracie). The distribution of gifts continued until finally all of the packages had been passed out.

"I guess that's it," said Gracie. She looked sadly at MacFarland and Rufus. "I'm sorry we didn't get anything for you guys."

MacFarland smiled. "Don't worry about it. Just being here is enough for us."

"Hey, what's that?" asked Harry, pointing beneath the tree.

Gracie leaned down and peered under the tree. "My gosh, you're right. There's another package there."

She struggled to pull it out of the tree, but finally

with Leroy's help, they extricated the object from the tree. Gracie put it on the floor in front of her. "I don't remember this one," she said, staring intently at the black plastic wrap of the package.

"Open it," said Gloria.

Gracie tore into the plastic, finally getting it off. The package consisted of a bundle wrapped in newspapers.

Gracie giggled. "Whoever gave this present didn't spare any expense, did they?" She unwrapped the paper, then gasped with surprise when she got the contents out.

It was bundles of money.

Everyone stared at the money in surprise.

"How much is there?" asked Harry.

Gracie and Kirk quickly counted the bundles of money. They looked at each other, then Gracie stared at each member of the group. "There's twenty-five thousand dollars here," she said in a whisper.

"We should split it up," said Leroy, "seven ways."

MacFarland shook his head. "No, no, if you're going to split it, split it five ways. It came from your tree."

As Gracie distributed five thousand dollars to each of the homeless people, MacFarland pulled Rufus to one side. "Just as I thought! The Smales brothers and Big Red were after the tree," he whispered. "They were using the trees, the ones with red sold tags, to identify where the payoff money was."

"Damn, boss, I think you're right."

"That money is evidence in a crime, Rufus. It should go back to the police."

"What are the police gonna do with it, boss? And remember when you found a bag of money in Peterson's house that he was going to give to those killers? Did you turn that in to the police?"

MacFarland hesitated, then smiled. "No, and I don't plan on turning this money in either. Everyone deserves a nice Christmas."

Gloria hugged her bundle of money next to her chest. "Hey, Harry, do you still think there's no such thing as Christmas magic?"

Harry held his share of the money in his hand, his face glowing. "I take it all back," he announced. "I said I didn't believe in Christmas magic, but now I do. With this, I'll be able to help my kids."

Everyone burst out laughing, then Gracie started singing a Christmas carol. Soon everyone was joining in.

When the party drew to a close, MacFarland and Rufus took their leave, wishing everyone a Merry Christmas and a Happy New Year. As they climbed into the truck, MacFarland smiled ruefully. "Rufus, who knew that a bunch of crooks could provide such Christmas cheer?"

"It's like you said, boss, at the Parade of Lights. If you have the Christmas spirit, it's always possible for some good to come out of any bad thing."

READ THE COMPLETE HOT DOG DETECTIVE SERIES

Homeless person...

Hot dog vendor...

Detective.

Follow Mark MacFarland as he helps solve the cases the police have given up on. The Hot Dog Detective mysteries are part cozy, part noir, set in the Mile High City of Denver.

THE AVID ANGLER

First in a the Hot Dog Detective series!

Betrayed by his wife and the system, former Denver Police Detective Mark MacFarland dropped out of the system...all the way. But now he has put drinking and homelessness behind him, bought a hot dog stand, and started a new life.

Then a noted defense lawyer asks MacFarland to prove that his client was wrongly accused of murdering her husband. Suddenly, MacFarland's past catches up with him.

Aided by his former partner, Cynthia Pierson, and his longtime homeless friend, Vietnam Vet Rufus, MacFarland discovers the husband's murder is actually part of a larger web of conspiracy...and may even tie in to the death of his wife.

THE GHOST IN THE CHRISTMAS STAR

Sally O'Brian pushed open the door to *EZ Pawn* and entered the cluttered store of her good friend, Sam Wasserman. Sam greeted her with enthusiasm.

"Sally, happy holidays to you! You have come for the Christmas ornaments?"

Sally held the door open for Matthew O'Brian, her husband. Matt didn't really need the door held for him. He could easily pass through the safety glass door, since Matt was a ghost. Matt had been killed earlier in the year in a fatal car crash that resulted when his car plunged fifty feet off a cliff into the Pacific Ocean. While he had died in the crash, Sally, his passenger, had miraculously survived.

Or so it had seemed. In fact, Sally had died also, but when both she and Matt arrived at an enormous Gate in an amorphous, ethereal place, the angel (or what they assumed was an angel) informed them that Matt could pass on, but Sally had to return back to the Earthly plane of existence. Reason? Only Heaven knew.

Matt wouldn't stand for losing the woman he loved, and contrary to the rules (yes, there were rules, though no one had thought of writing them down), he returned with Sally. She was brought back from the brink of death by her doctor son-in-law, Jack Winston, and Matt returned as a ghost.

Since that fateful day, Sally could see and talk to ghosts.

It was a blessing and a curse. A blessing, because it meant she could keep talking to Matthew; a curse, because it meant she had an obligation to help ghosts trapped on the Earthly plane to pass on. She had recently done just that, helping a mother and daughter find peace after death.

But now it was December. Sally wanted nothing more than to fix up the three buildings that made up the Dolphin Point Bed and Breakfast. The largest of the homes was the Cliff House, a spectacular home built on the edge of the cliff overlooking the Pacific. The second home was the Blue House, a smaller, but cozier home. The third was the Cabin, a rustic one room getaway fantasy home on the furthest part of Dolphin Point. At the current moment, only the Cliff House had been made rental ready.

But Sally wasn't satisfied with that. She wanted to dress up the Cliff House with all sorts of Christmas decorations. The problem was, she had spent all of her budget on furniture, accessories, and furnishings for the house.

She had mentioned to Sam a week earlier that if he came across any Christmas decorations, she would be interested in them.

And, true to the spirit of Christmas miracles, Sam had come through.

"I bought the estate of a guy named Brett Cosgrove. You might have heard of him. I think he was a Hollywood movie star, retired here in Crystal Cove, and took up stage theatrics."

"I've heard of him," said Matt. "I wouldn't call him a movie star, though. I was under the impression he was a stunt man."

Sally listened to her husband, aware that Sam could not hear a word Matt said. "Did Mr. Cosgrove recently die?"

Sam nodded. "His son, Simon Cosgrove, cleaned out the entire house, packed everything in a shipping container, and sold it to me. You need more furniture?"

Sally smiled. "I will at some point. Where are the Christmas decorations?"

"Over here," said Sam. "I can help you move them to your car if you're parked out front."

"I would appreciate that, Sam."

As Sally and Sam carried the boxes out to Sally's car, Sam gave her one last warning. "Be careful, Sally. I think I mentioned that the ornaments might be haunted."

Sally laughed. "Surely you don't believe in ghosts, Sam."

"I don't," said Sam, staring at her intently. "But I hear you do."

THE TAROT READER

Tia Chamas moved to Arcana Glen to help her grandmother run her shop, *Tea & Tarot*. When a handsome stranger turns on New Year Day for a Tarot reading, Tia doesn't expect her weak magic to be good enough to receive a real prophecy. To her shock, she has a terrible vision that warns her that her mystery guest is an Elf Prince, and his life is in danger. She vows to do whatever she must to save him.

She didn't *intend* to magically bind him to her side!

THE ELF PRINCE

Delson Norion has been in exile and hiding among mundanes for ten years. He's come to the small mountain town of Arcana Glen for one reason: To assassinate the murderous Magician who killed Delson's aunt and helped kill his parents. When Tia, a beautiful witch, traps him with her spell, at first all he wants is to break the binding. Even if he survives his dangerous mission, he is obligated to marry an Elf Princess, not a human Tarot reader.

But when he realizes that enemies are trying to kill Tia, Delson's priorities change. Now he has more reason than ever to slay the evil wizard...to protect the woman he can never have.

This tale is a stand-alone HEA love story set in the same town and time as The Magician & the Fool, with some overlapping characters.

Read the entire novella for FREE!

Or click her to buy and Read The Tarot Reader's New Year Promise.

THE FOOL

Bethany Dilly was a fool, and she knew it. What woman would agree to an arranged marriage to a man she'd never met? Even if he was gorgeous, sexy, talented, and mysterious, a famous Las Vegas Magician, and a billionaire who lived in an honest-to-gosh castle in the remote mountain town of Arcana Glen in the Rocky Mountains. Rumors swirled around him that his previous six wives had all vanished under mysterious circumstances.

But Bethany agreed to become Wife Seven to save the life of her best friend.

THE MAGICIAN

Alephander Guiscard's secret to success as a Magician is simple—his magic is real. He is, in fact, the most powerful wizard, not only on Earth, but in all the Seven Mortal Spheres. He is the last of the twenty-two Guardians who once warded the Gates between the

Elven, Angel, and Demon realms and the Mundane Human world.

After keeping a vow of silence for nearly a century, Alephander is on the verge of his greatest triumph. The only catch is that to complete his most magnificent spell yet, he must find a wife who can go an entire year without speaking. This is his last chance. He needs a woman who is somber, quiet, and above all, obedient.

Bethany, his latest bride, is NOT that woman.

ABOUT MATHIYA ADAMS

After living for more than twenty years in the Denver Metro area, I have relocated to Southern California, where the free and easy lifestyle has inspired me...to search for a cozier place to live!

I've chosen Crystal Cove, a small town on the coast of Northern California

As you may realize, Crystal Cove is fictional, but it is based on several of the California Coastal towns that I have visited and enjoyed over the years: Monterrey, La Jolla, Carmel by the Sea, San Juan Capistrano, Morro Bay, and many others. For, if truth be known, I grew up in Southern California and it will once again be the primary locale for future stories.

Email me at Misque Press: editor@misquepress.com or get on my mailing list at www.mathiyaadams.com.